Virtues of a Great Warrior
Ori Avnur

Contact information:

Website: www.inspiringreads4kids.com
Facebook: Inspiring Reads for Kids
Email: info@inspiringreads4kids.com

ISBN-13: 978-1541246836
ISBN-10: 1541246837

INSPIRING REaDS FOR KIDS

To receive info about new releases, promotions and freebies, you can register to our free newsletter
www.inspiringreads4kids.com

Virtues of a Great Warrior

Written and Illustrated by Ori Avnur

Translated by Ram Avnur and Sarah Jane Griffiths

I am called *Water That Cannot Dry.*
I was born in the Kingdom of Xiang.

I was destined to inherit my parent's farm but I wished to acquire the secret skills of swordsmanship.

At an early age I left, I was determined to realize my wish and learn the virtues of a great warrior.

After twenty-one years of practice, I reached greatness in the art of the sword, thus I was permitted audience with a great master.

The great master gazed into my eyes and said: "In our kingdom live three thieves, powerful and very dangerous. It is your destiny to meet them in battle. The encounter with each of the three, shall make you face death and teach you an important lesson."

The Battle with *Ice That Cannot Melt*

I confronted the mighty thief *Ice That Cannot Melt* upon the Bamboo Island at the Southern Realm.

We fought for three days and three nights, in the end I won.

I disarmed him of his sword and turned to end his life. Yet something hindered me. I looked deep into his eyes and then I knew, I may not take life.

Returning to my great master, I told him of what befell me. "Master, I know not if I have failed you. What warrior am I if I cannot kill?"

The master fell silent for a while, finally, gazing into my eyes he said: "Much must you learn before facing *Fire That Cannot Be Extinguished*."

The battle with *Fire That Cannot Be Extinguished*

Ten years passed since my encounter with the first thief, and the time came for me to confront *Fire That Cannot Be Extinguished* upon the Snowy Mountains at the Northern Realm.

We fought for six days and six nights.

At last, after great effort, I won. My sword stood but a touch from his throat. His eyes met mine. Again I knew - I may not take life.

"I have defeated you *Fire That Cannot Be Extinguished*" I said. "I can end your life now, yet I choose not to." I put my sword aside and extended my hand. "Giving you a second chance is a greater virtue than executing you. You are free, go now and forsake the path of the sword!"

Once again, returning to my great master, I told him what befell me. "Master, I know not if I have failed you. What warrior am I if I cannot kill?"

The master replied: "Much must you learn before facing *Rock That Cannot Crumble*."

Ten strenuous years of training passed before I came face to face with the mightiest of all thieves, *Rock That Cannot Crumble*.

We confronted one another upon the Endless Desert Lands of the Western Realm,

and for eight days and eight nights neither of us
moved.

On the ninth day *Rock That Cannot Crumble* moved first. He stepped slowly towards me and bowed.

"Coming here, it was clear to me I would kill you" he said, "yet one long look into your eyes revealed to me that I no longer desire killing."

Returning to my great master for the third time, he told me:

"In your first battle you did well, the great warrior whispered within your heart, the one who trains to prevent killing. Yet you were too young to understand what was whispered.

Well you did in your second battle too, you learned to hear the great warrior who lies within you. He does not train to take life away, but to give it back to those who lost their way.

And you did well indeed in your third battle, you learned that true victory is accomplished when the sword is no longer needed. You have gained the virtues of the great warrior:

His skills are great as he is swift, he is strong as he is still, yet his heart knows mercy. He is wise enough to choose life
- he removes the sword from his enemy's hands.

He stands his ground, yet does not surrender to vengeance. His eyes see far beyond the sword. He brings life back where it was forgotten
- he removes the sword from his enemy's mind.

He possesses the life-giving force of healing. He is true to a cause higher than war. Through his presence he shows the path of light
- he removes the sword from his enemy's heart.

And now *Water That Cannot Dry*, you are no longer an ordinary warrior. On this day you have become a great master, and there are three men who wish to learn from you."

Three figures entered the dojo and bowed. When they stepped into the light I recognized their faces, the three thieves of the Kingdom of Xiang.

That day, I laid down my sword forever.

The End

You don't know how far just a few words can reach! If your child enjoyed this book, please help us reach other family's hearts by leaving a review on Amazon. Thank you so much!

INSPIRING READS FOR KIDS

About the author

Ori Avnur is a meditation teacher and an artist from Israel. He began his career as an art teacher for children. Later on he moved to live in the east to study meditation and eastern philosophies for more than a decade. During this period of meditation practices, he began to write his children's stories and founded "Inspiring Reads for Kids". Today he is running a drawing and animation school for children while writing and publishing his children's books.

Recently his books have been recommended by some of the most influential meditation, mindfulness and spirituality teachers of our time, among them Ven. Jetsunma Tenzin Palmo, the most senior Western Tibetan Buddhist nun alive. You can read Ven. Jetsunma Tenzin Palmo's words about Ori's books in the testimonial section of our website.

Second book of your choice for free!

Choose your second illustrated digital book with narration and uplifting music from our collection. Please write to **info@inspiringreads4kids.com** with proof of purchase.

We also offer a monthly subscription with printed & digital books with narration and uplifting music plus mindful & meditative activities for children. For more info please visit **www.inspiringreads4kids.com**

Some of our books by Ori Avnur:

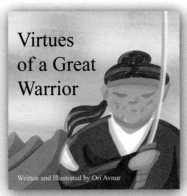

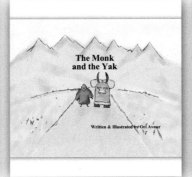

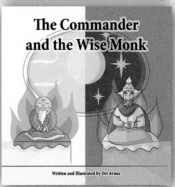

Made in the USA
Monee, IL
06 March 2021